Matthew Gollub ◆ pictures by Leovigildo Martinez

THE TWENTY-FIVE MIXTEC CATS

TAMBOURINE BOOKS ◆ NEW YORK

Printed in Hong Kong by South China Printing Company (1988) Ltd

Library of Congress Cataloging in Publication Data

Gollub, Matthew. The twenty-five Mixtec cats/by Matthew Gollub;
illustrated by Leovigildo Martinez.—1st ed. p. cm.
Summary: The inhabitants of a mountain village are suspicious of
the twenty-five cats who come to live with their healer, until the
cats are able to help lift a curse placed on the butcher.
[1. Cats—Fiction.   2. Mexico—Fiction.   3. Magic—Fiction.]
I. Martinez, Leovigildo, ill.   II. Title.
PZ7.G583Tw 1993 [E]—dc20   92-13585 CIP AC
ISBN 0-688-11639-6. — ISBN 0-688-11640-X (lib. bdg.)
3   5   7   9   10   8   6   4   2
First edition

To Ian and Tully   M.G.
To the people of *La Mixteca*   L.M.

With thanks to our friends, Patrick Dickson and
Nancy Mayagoitia, and to all who helped
make this collaboration possible.

There once was a healer who lived alone in a village high in the mountains. You would never see any cats in his village. Not a single one lived there, for it was hot during the day, cold at night, and dusty all the time. It was not a comfortable place for cats—or for anyone else.

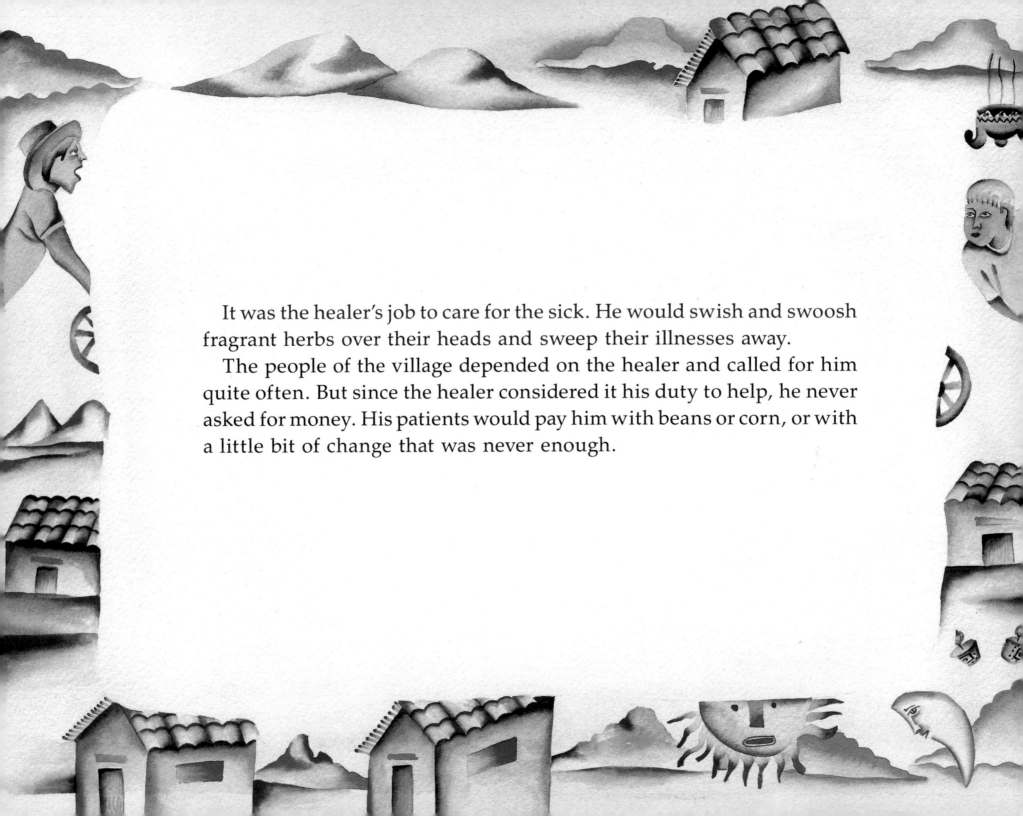

It was the healer's job to care for the sick. He would swish and swoosh fragrant herbs over their heads and sweep their illnesses away.

The people of the village depended on the healer and called for him quite often. But since the healer considered it his duty to help, he never asked for money. His patients would pay him with beans or corn, or with a little bit of change that was never enough.

One day, the healer went to a Mixtec market where a woman offered to give him twenty-five kittens. Since the healer was always short of money, and since no one in his village had ever had a cat, he carried the kittens home in a pillowcase to sell them door to door.

"How could we raise a cat?" scoffed his neighbors. "It's so hot and cold and dusty here. Besides, we don't have food for cats. It's hard enough just to feed our children."

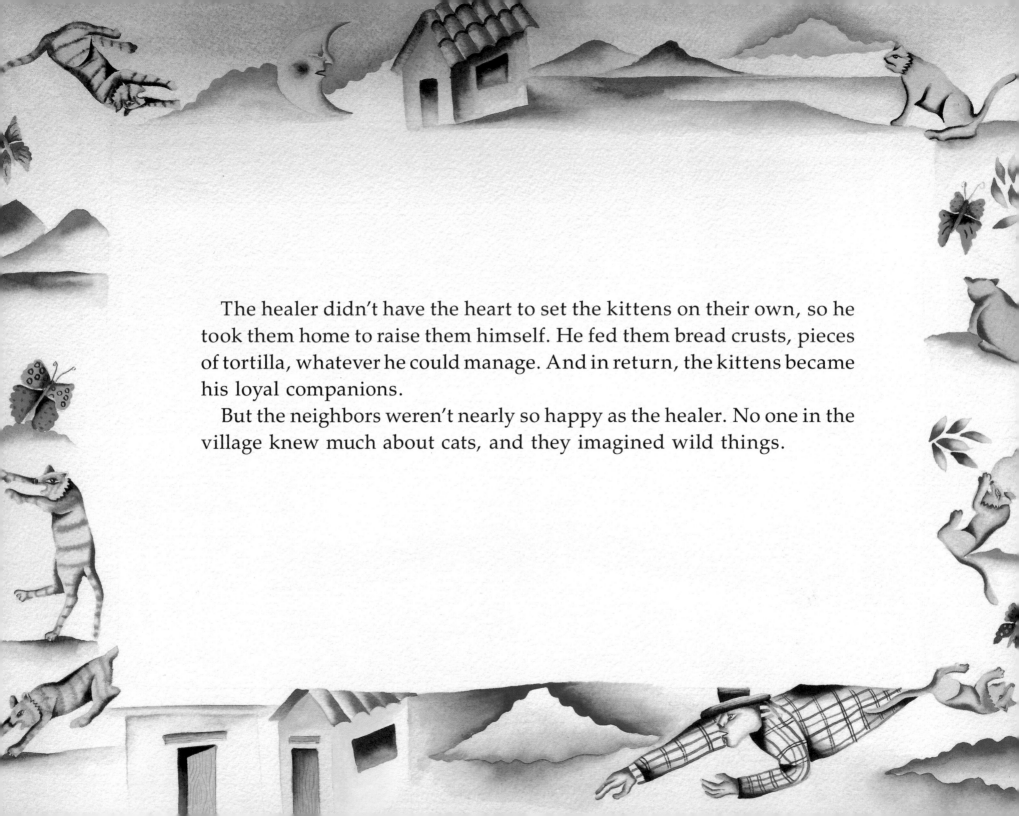

The healer didn't have the heart to set the kittens on their own, so he took them home to raise them himself. He fed them bread crusts, pieces of tortilla, whatever he could manage. And in return, the kittens became his loyal companions.

But the neighbors weren't nearly so happy as the healer. No one in the village knew much about cats, and they imagined wild things.

"They'll eat all my flour," bemoaned the baker, "then how will I go about baking bread?"

"Cats don't eat flour," said the butcher woman. "They eat mice, but also cows!"

"And to keep warm at night," cried the hatmaker and the florist, "they'll set fire to our fields!"

The neighbors marched to the healer's home and pounded on the door. "You must get rid of those filthy rodents," pronounced the butcher. "They make too much noise. We've heard the way they meow. And it's only a matter of time before they eat up all our food."

The healer felt it was important to get along with his neighbors. "The kittens will stay by my side," he promised. "They won't cause any trouble."

Soon the healer was known for his helpers, the twenty-five Mixtec cats. The kittens, which were growing up, learned to help him swish and swoosh. But still the neighbors gossiped by the well.

"Have you seen how big the cats have grown?"

"At this rate, they'll soon be the size of *burros*!"

"The cats are evil!" wailed the butcher. "So we must go to the evil healer!"

The evil healer lived outside the village. She lived all alone, the way the good healer used to, but devoted herself to very different work. It was this healer's business to cast evil spells.

When the neighbors paid her to get rid of the cats, she looked over her collection of magic things: poisonous herbs, a toucan's beak, even the skeleton of a rattlesnake. "No," she reconsidered. "I'll send messengers. That way no one will know I was responsible."

That night she flew through a haunted wood in search of her coyotes.
She pointed toward where the healer lived, and the pack trotted off as if
in a trance.

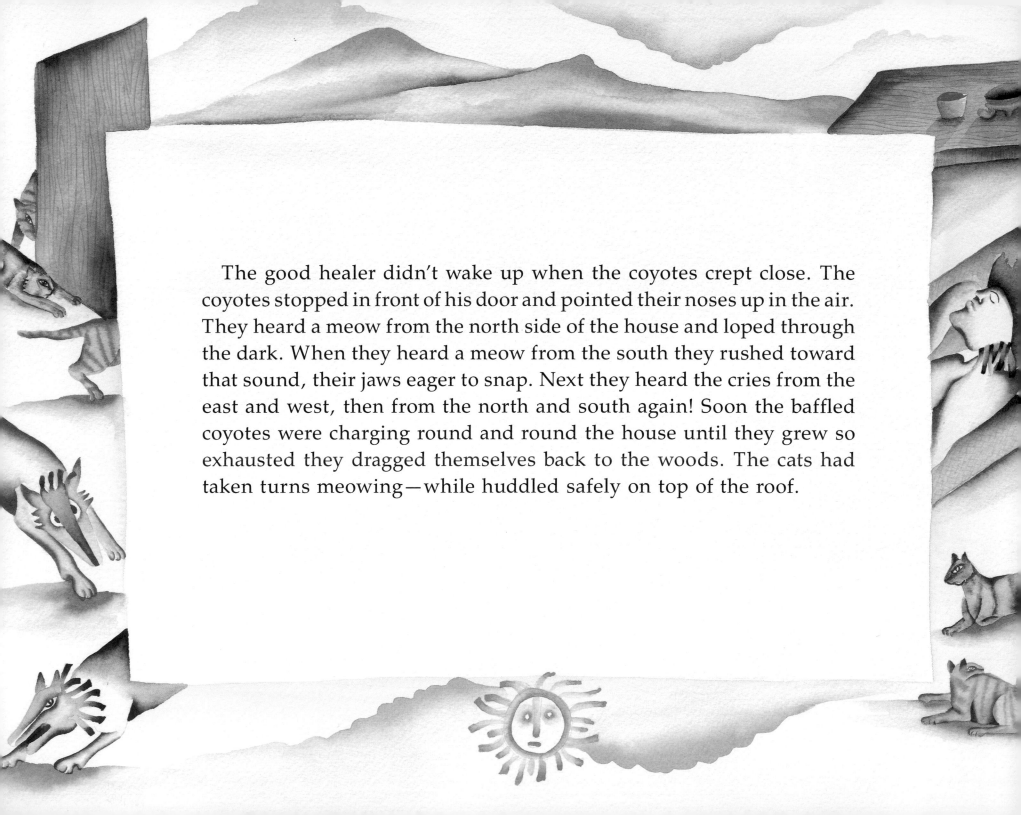

The good healer didn't wake up when the coyotes crept close. The coyotes stopped in front of his door and pointed their noses up in the air. They heard a meow from the north side of the house and loped through the dark. When they heard a meow from the south they rushed toward that sound, their jaws eager to snap. Next they heard the cries from the east and west, then from the north and south again! Soon the baffled coyotes were charging round and round the house until they grew so exhausted they dragged themselves back to the woods. The cats had taken turns meowing—while huddled safely on top of the roof.

The next morning when the cats followed the healer out to his field, the neighbors could not believe their eyes.

The butcher led the neighbors back to the evil healer. "We demand our money," she announced.

The evil healer tilted her head. "What nonsense is this?"

"You're nothing but a fake," said the butcher. "You can't even do away with twenty-five cats! You have no special powers."

The evil healer thrust her twisted fingers forward and glared into the butcher's eyes.

"We'll see who has no special powers," she menaced.

The following day, the butcher fell ill. The pain began with an ache in her gut. Then she felt flashes of hot and cold. She felt so dizzy that the meats in her stall began spinning before her eyes. She closed the stall and went home to lie down and couldn't get up for a day.

Two days passed and she didn't feel better. Her fever would not break, and she started to grow gaunt. The neighbors knew that unless they got help the butcher would not recover. They went to the good healer's home and described the sickness.

"It is hard," he said, "to cure a person of a curse. But, it is my duty to try."

The healer arrived at the butcher's home with his twenty-five cats. He arranged his sacred water, rosemary, and rue, while the cats swept out the house. He sprinkled the herbs with drops of the water and began to swish and swoosh. He and the cats repeated the process, but the butcher only moaned.

"Cats," the healer told them, "my powers alone are not enough. All of you must do as I do if we are to rid the butcher of evil."

The healer got the cats in position. Then, at his signal, he and the cats inhaled. They drew in a breath of air so hard it rustled the butcher's hair. As they held the breath of air in their mouths, the butcher began to recover! Color returned to her pallid face, and the pain in her gut was lifted!

"Bravo!" shouted the neighbors.

But then they noticed the healer's face. He could not exhale. The evil had left the butcher but now was stuck inside *him*! The cats, who were much smaller, could spit out the evil and continue to breathe. But the healer's cheeks were fast turning blue. Who would heal the healer?

The butcher got up to let the healer lie down. The neighbors looked on helplessly as the healer's hair turned gray and limp.

Suddenly, one cat leapt out the window and, in an eye's wink, ran to the evil healer's house. He snatched the evil healer's mask off her table and slipped out the door before she could shout.

He dragged it back to the home of the butcher. The other cats helped him pull it onto the roof. They dropped the clay mask over the ledge and watched it shatter on the ground.

At that instant the healer, sprawled on the mat, let out a tremendous gasp of air. His breath created a gust of wind that whipped around the room and wafted out the window.

The neighbors cheered with great relief. The cats had not only helped the butcher but saved the healer as well.

The butcher, florist, hatmaker, and baker now accepted them once and for all.

The Mixtec cats became heroes in the village as word of their brave deeds spread. To this day, the butcher gives them scraps of meat, and the baker feeds them bread. And the Mixtec cats play by the healer's side and make sure his house is clean.

A NOTE ABOUT THE ARTIST

Leovigildo Martinez comes from Oaxaca (wa-HAH-kah), a state in southern Mexico known for its richly artistic atmosphere. Oaxaca has seventeen ethnic minorities, many of whom speak different languages and dialects. This unusual mix of so many indigenous peoples has created a remarkable array of art, folklore, and crafts. Fiestas, folk customs, and even the textiles of the region find their way into Mr. Martinez's paintings, contributing to a genre that he describes as "figurative magic."

The illustrations in this book are watercolors on textured paper. Glaze was used to achieve the distinctive shades of color. The elements that recur in Mr. Martinez's work are used to symbolize life in Oaxacan villages, particularly within the Mixtec and Zapotec cultures. His first major show in the United States took place in 1992 at the Santa Fe East gallery in New Mexico. Thirteen of Mr. Martinez's works are on permanent display at the Museum of Latin American Art in Uruguay.

A note regarding pronunciation: "Mixtec" is pronounced variably as Mees-tec, Meesh-tec, Mis-tec, and Mish-tec. Mixtec dialects and the influence of Spanish account for these subtle differences. Please choose that which sounds best to you and have fun reading aloud!